THE SMURFS

Peyo

Gargamel had captured Smurfette and had smurfed her into a cage! Undeterred by the danger, I went, alone, to challenge that infernal sorcerer...
Ooooh!
Oooh!
Pff ...What baloney!

PAPERCUTZ™
NEW YORK

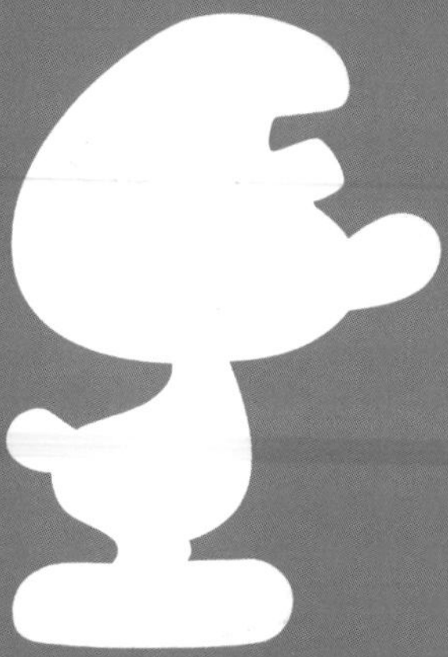

THE SMURFS TALES #3

"Brainy Smurf's Walk"
BY PEYO
WITH THE COLLABORATION OF ALAIN JOST FOR THE SCRIPT, JEROEN DE CONNICK FOR THE ARTWORK, PAOLO MADDALENI FOR THE COLORS

"Challenges for Hefty Smurf"
BY PEYO
WITH THE COLLABORATION OF LUC PARTHEONS FOR THE SCRIPT, ALAIN MAURY FOR THE ARTWORK, PAOLO MADDALENI FOR THE COLORS

"Clumsy Smurf's Dragonfly"
BY PEYO
WITH THE COLLABORATION OF LUC PARTHEONS FOR THE SCRIPT, LAURENT CAGNAIT FOR THE ARTWORK, PAOLO MADDALENI FOR THE COLORS

"The Squash Smurfs"
BY PEYO
WITH THE COLLABORATION OF LUC PARTHEONS FOR THE SCRIPT, ALAIN MAURY FOR THE ARTWORK, PAOLO MADDALENI FOR THE COLORS

"Smurflily Strange World"
BY PEYO
WITH THE COLLABORATION OF ALAIN JOST FOR FOR THE SCRIPT, MIGUEL DIAZ FOR THE ARTWORK, PAOLO MADDALENI FOR THE COLORS

"The Betrayal of Smurfblossom"
BY PEYO
WITH THE COLLABORATION OF LUC PARTHEONS FOR THE SCRIPT, ALAIN MAURY FOR THE ARTWORK, PAOLO MADDALENI FOR THE COLORS

"The Crow in Smurfy Grove"
BY PEYO
WITH THE COLLABORATION OF LUC PARTHEONS FOR THE SCRIPT, ALAIN MAURY FOR THE ARTWORK, PAOLO MADDALENI FOR THE COLORS

"The Paper Smurfs"
BY PEYO

"Spiders Attack at Dawn"
BY PEYO

"The Thousand Crowns"
BY PEYO

Joe Johnson, *SMURFLATIONS*
Bryan Senka, *LETTERING SMURF*
Janice Chiang, *LETTERING SMURF*
Calvin Louie, *LETTERING ASSISTANT SMURF*
Léa Zimmerman, *SMURFIC PRODUCTION*
Matt. Murray, *SMURF CONSULTANT*
Lily Lu , Jordan Hillman, *SMURF INTERNS*
Jeff Whitman, *MANAGING SMURF*
Jim Salicrup, *SMURF-IN-CHIEF*

HC ISBN 978-1-5458-0756-9
PB ISBN 978-1-5458-0757-6

PRINTED IN MALAYSIA
DECEMBER 2021

Papercutz books may be purchased for business or promotional use. For information on bulk purchases please contact Macmillan Corporate and Premium Sales Department at (800) 221-7945 x5442.

DISTRIBUTED BY MACMILLAN
FIRST PAPERCUTZ PRINTING

MEET THE SMURFS OF SMURFY GROVE

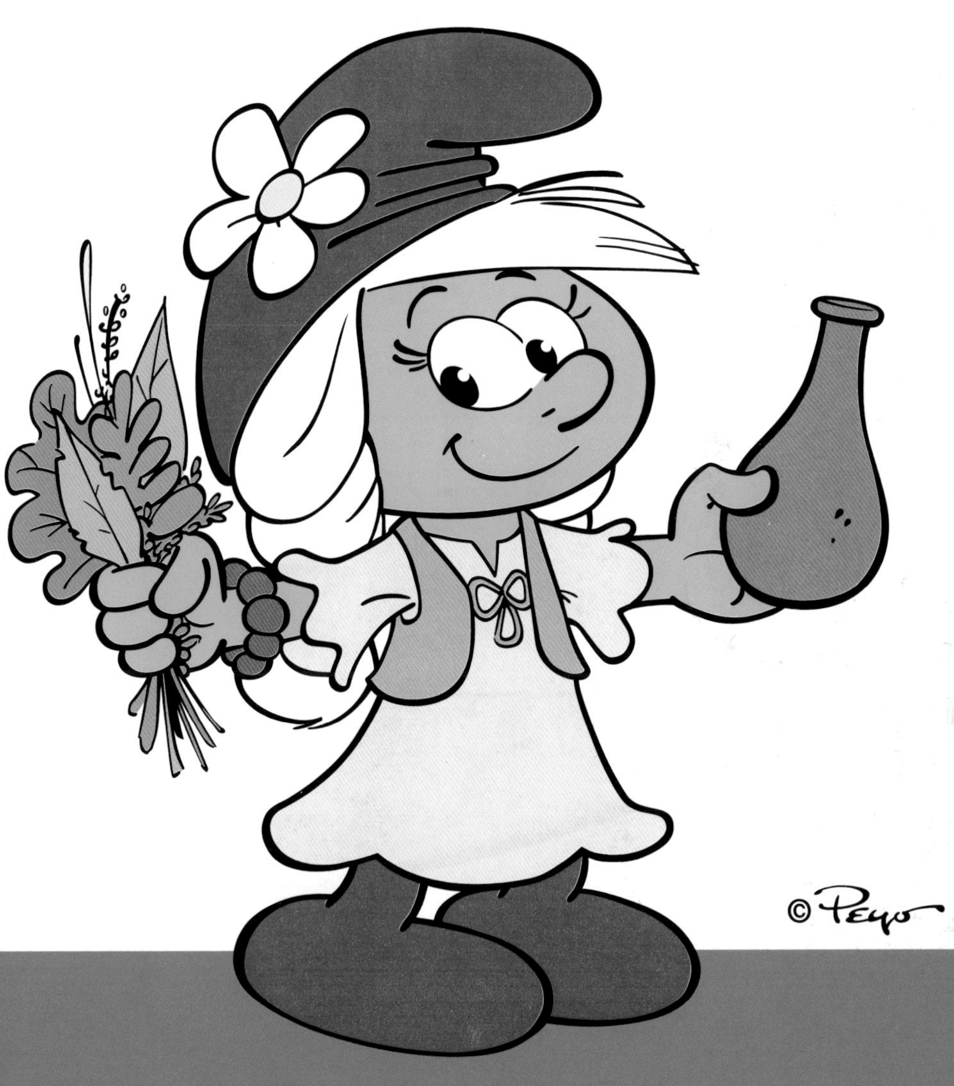
© Peyo

SMURFWILLOW (WILLOW)

Smurfwillow is the magnanimous leader of Smurfy Grove. The decision-maker of the group, Willow has raised her girls to be tough warriors, ready for whatever dangers they may face in the forest. She also has great knowledge of plants and botany, mixing flowers into potions to create healing elixirs.

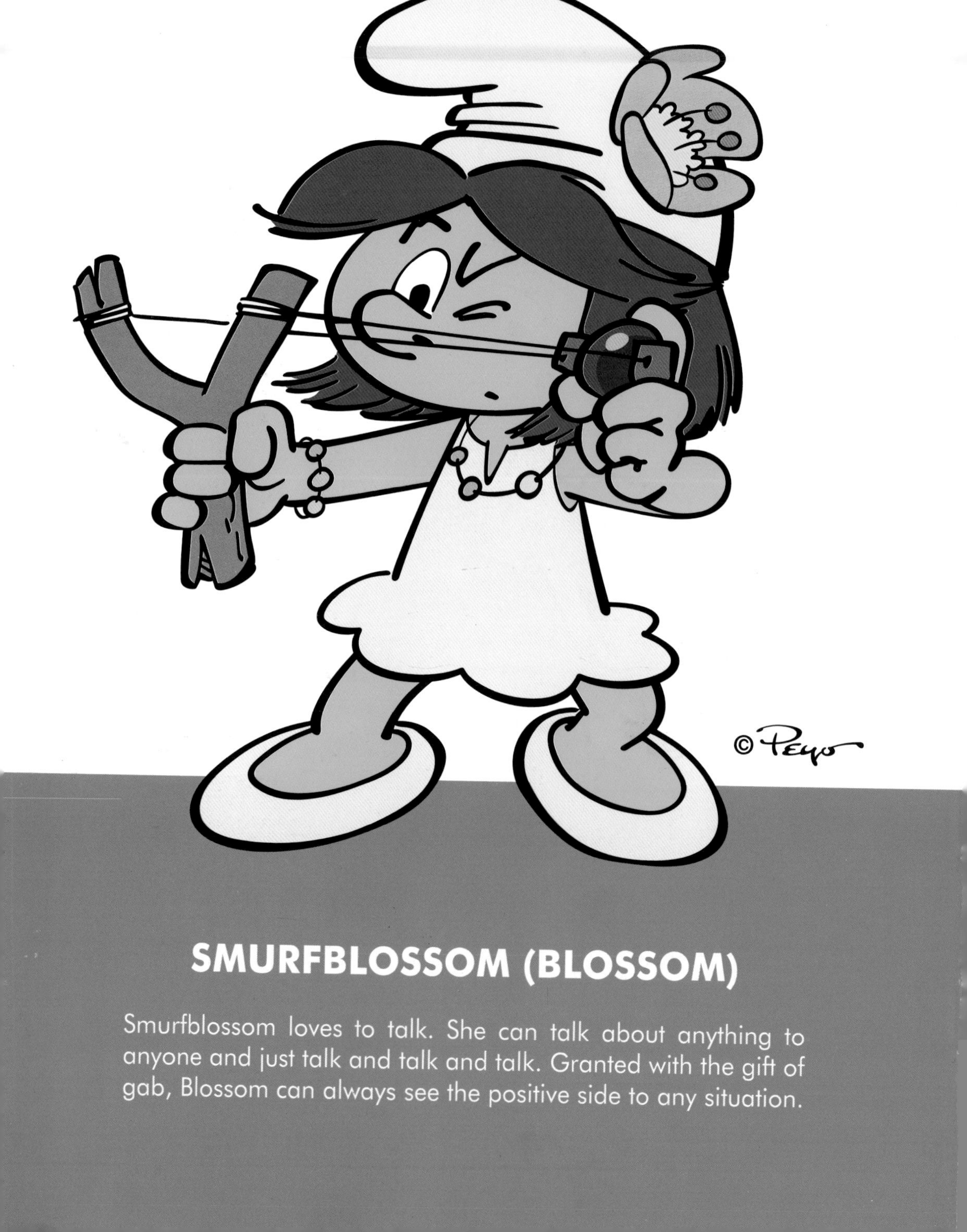
© Peyo

SMURFBLOSSOM (BLOSSOM)

Smurfblossom loves to talk. She can talk about anything to anyone and just talk and talk and talk. Granted with the gift of gab, Blossom can always see the positive side to any situation.

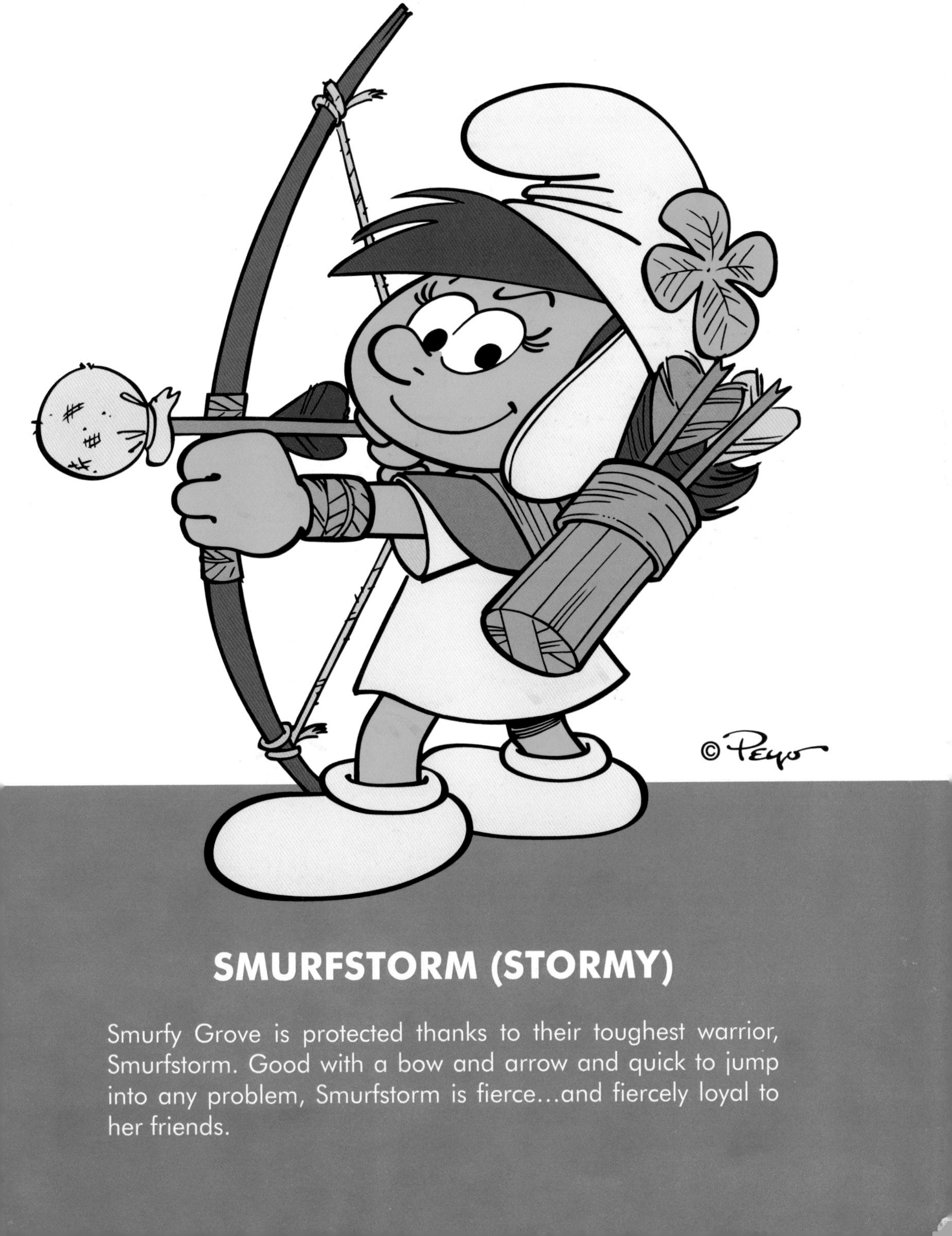
© Peyo

SMURFSTORM (STORMY)

Smurfy Grove is protected thanks to their toughest warrior, Smurfstorm. Good with a bow and arrow and quick to jump into any problem, Smurfstorm is fierce...and fiercely loyal to her friends.

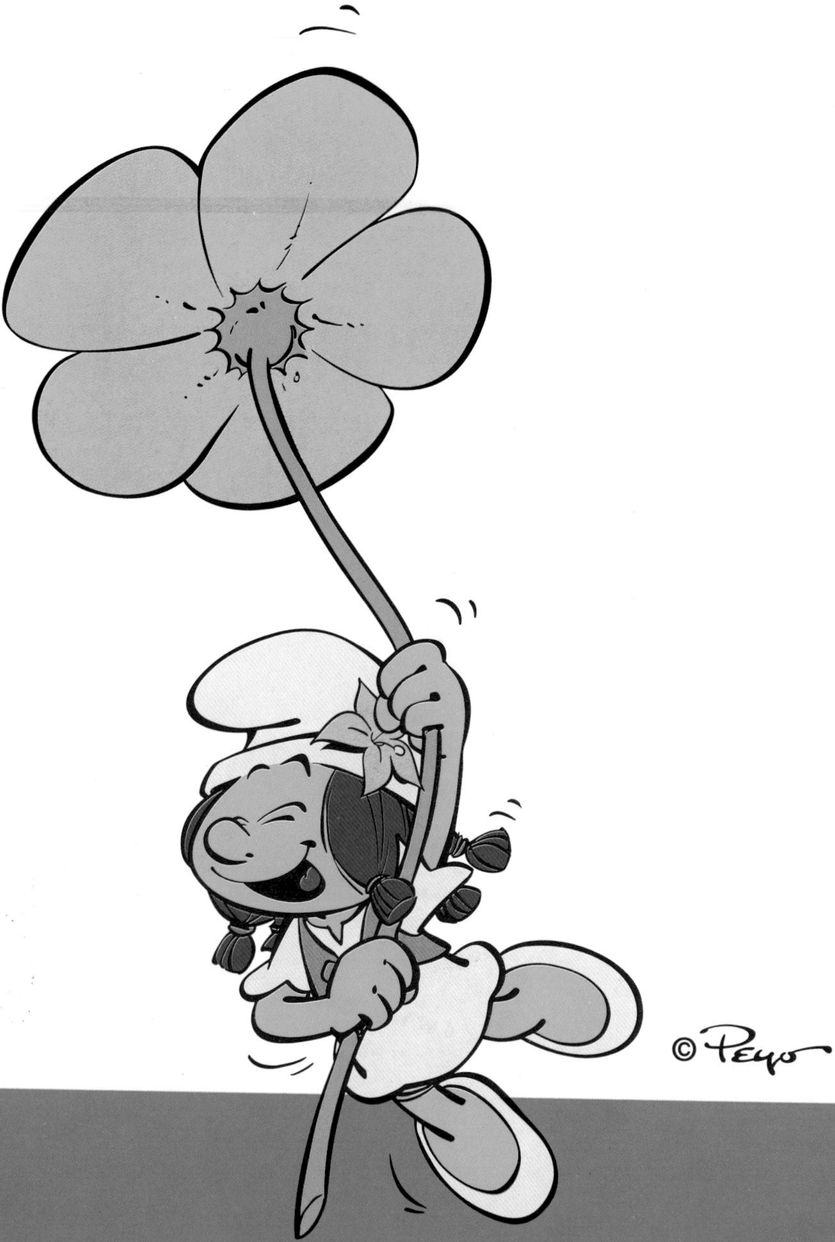
© Peyo

SMURFLILY (LILY)

Smurflily is smart, sassy, and practical. She can be outspoken and at times disagrees with the rest of Smurfy Grove, but she always wants what is best for her sisters.

THE VILLAGE BEHIND THE WALL

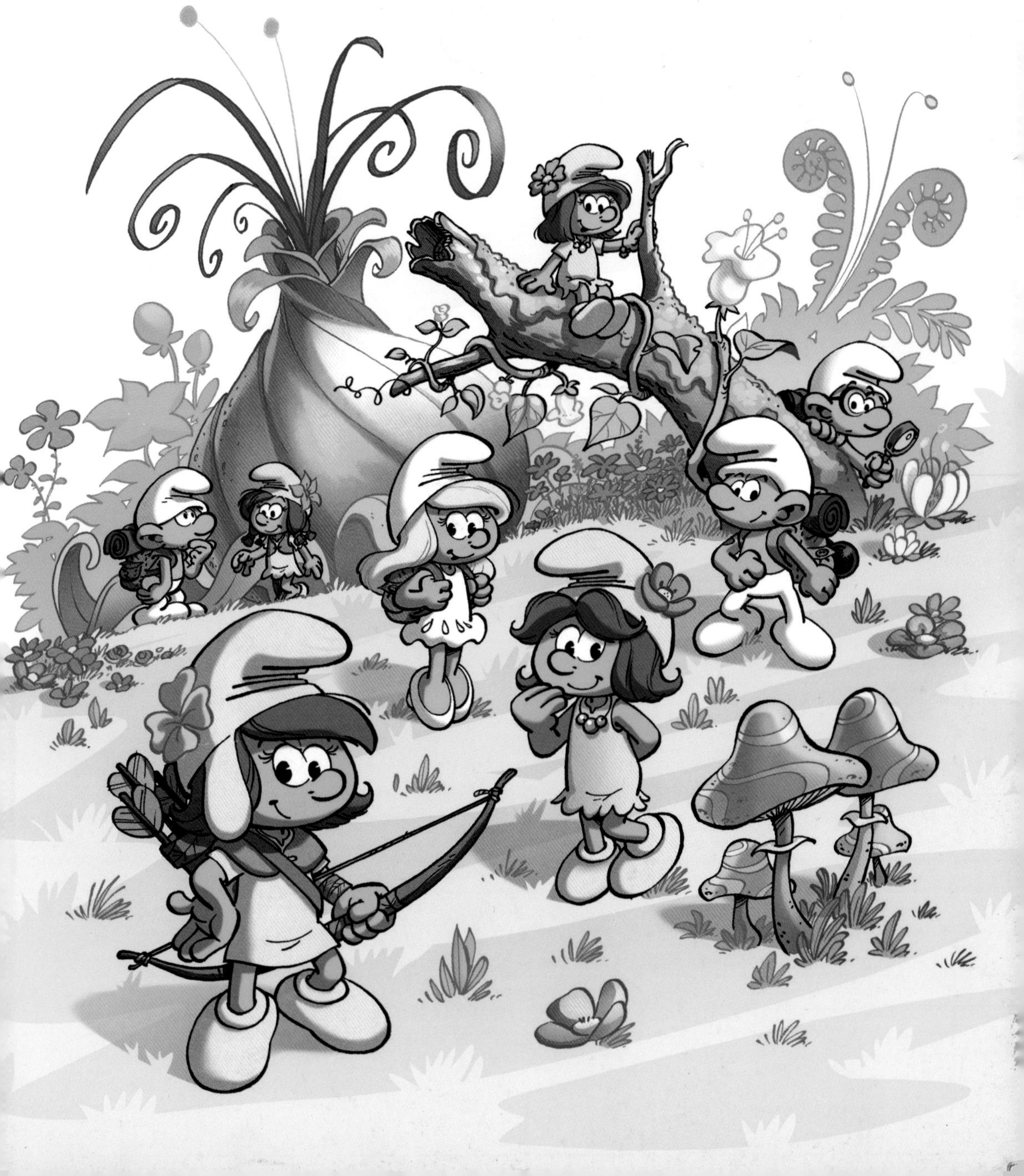

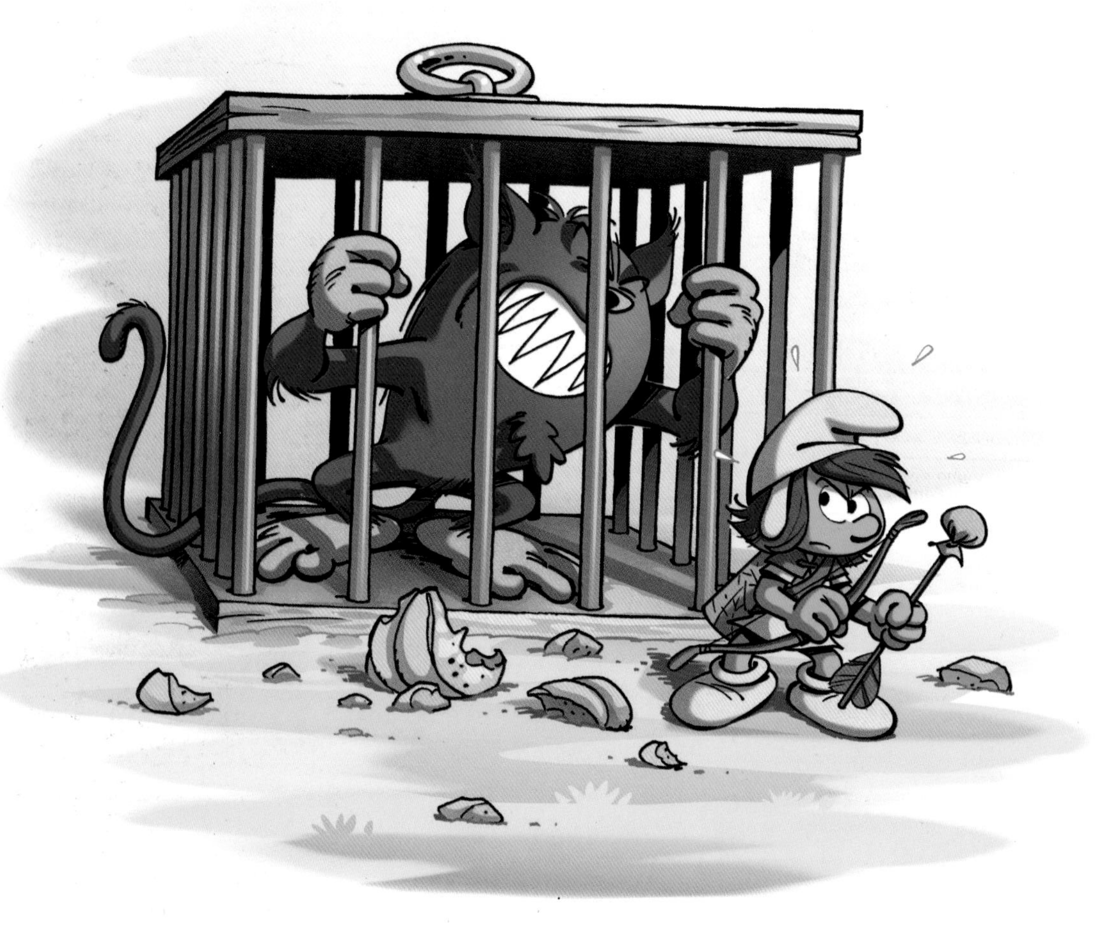

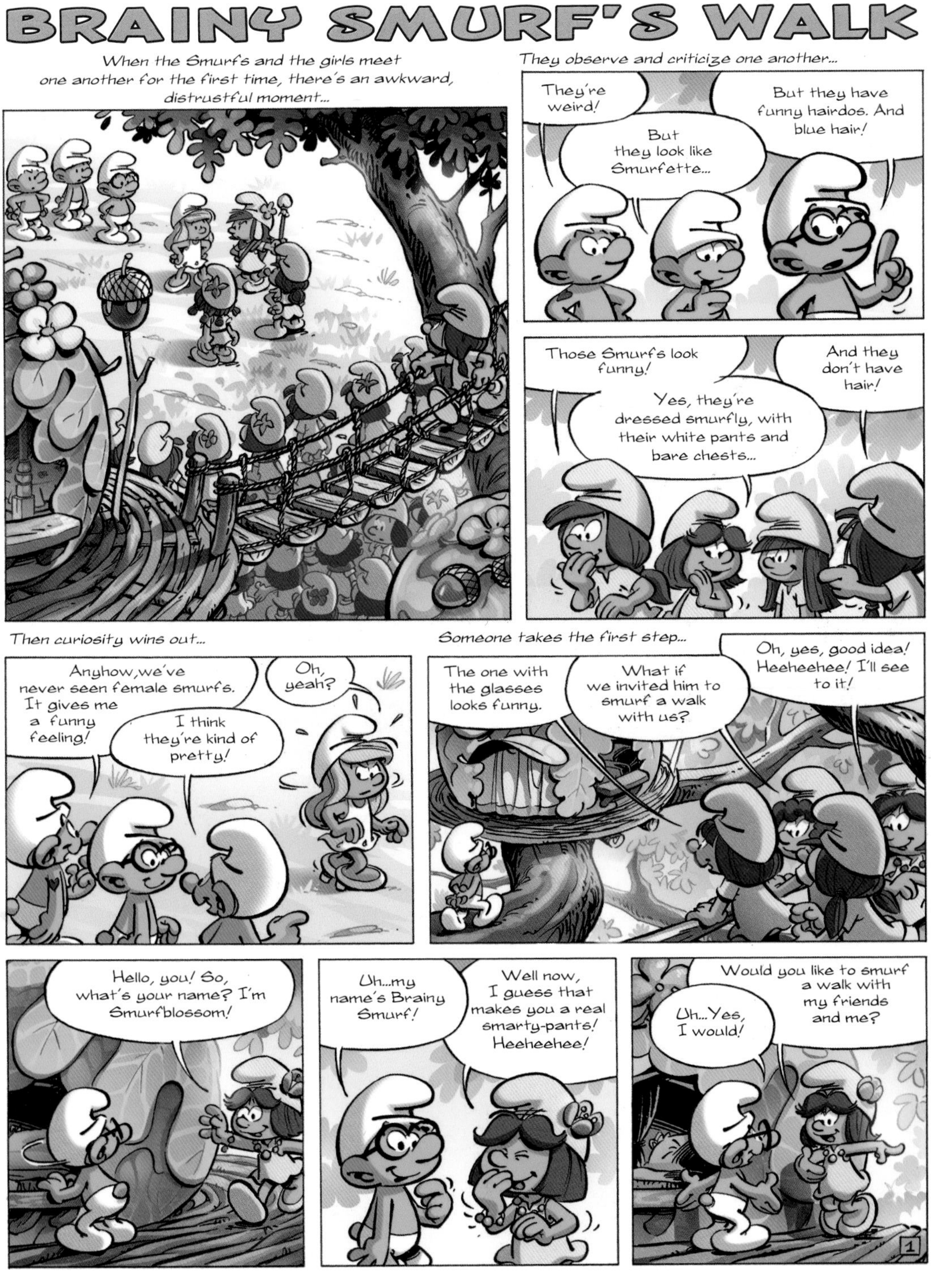
BRAINY SMURF'S WALK
When the Smurfs and the girls meet one another for the first time, there's an awkward, distrustful moment...
They observe and criticize one another...
They're weird!
But they look like Smurfette...
But they have funny hairdos. And blue hair!
Those Smurfs look funny!
Yes, they're dressed smurfly, with their white pants and bare chests...
And they don't have hair!
Then curiosity wins out...
Anyhow, we've never seen female smurfs. It gives me a funny feeling!
I think they're kind of pretty!
Oh, yeah?
Someone takes the first step...
The one with the glasses looks funny.
What if we invited him to smurf a walk with us?
Oh, yes, good idea! Heeheehee! I'll see to it!
Hello, you! So, what's your name? I'm Smurfblossom!
Uh...my name's Brainy Smurf!
Well now, I guess that makes you a real smarty-pants! Heeheehee!
Would you like to smurf a walk with my friends and me?
Uh...Yes, I would!
1

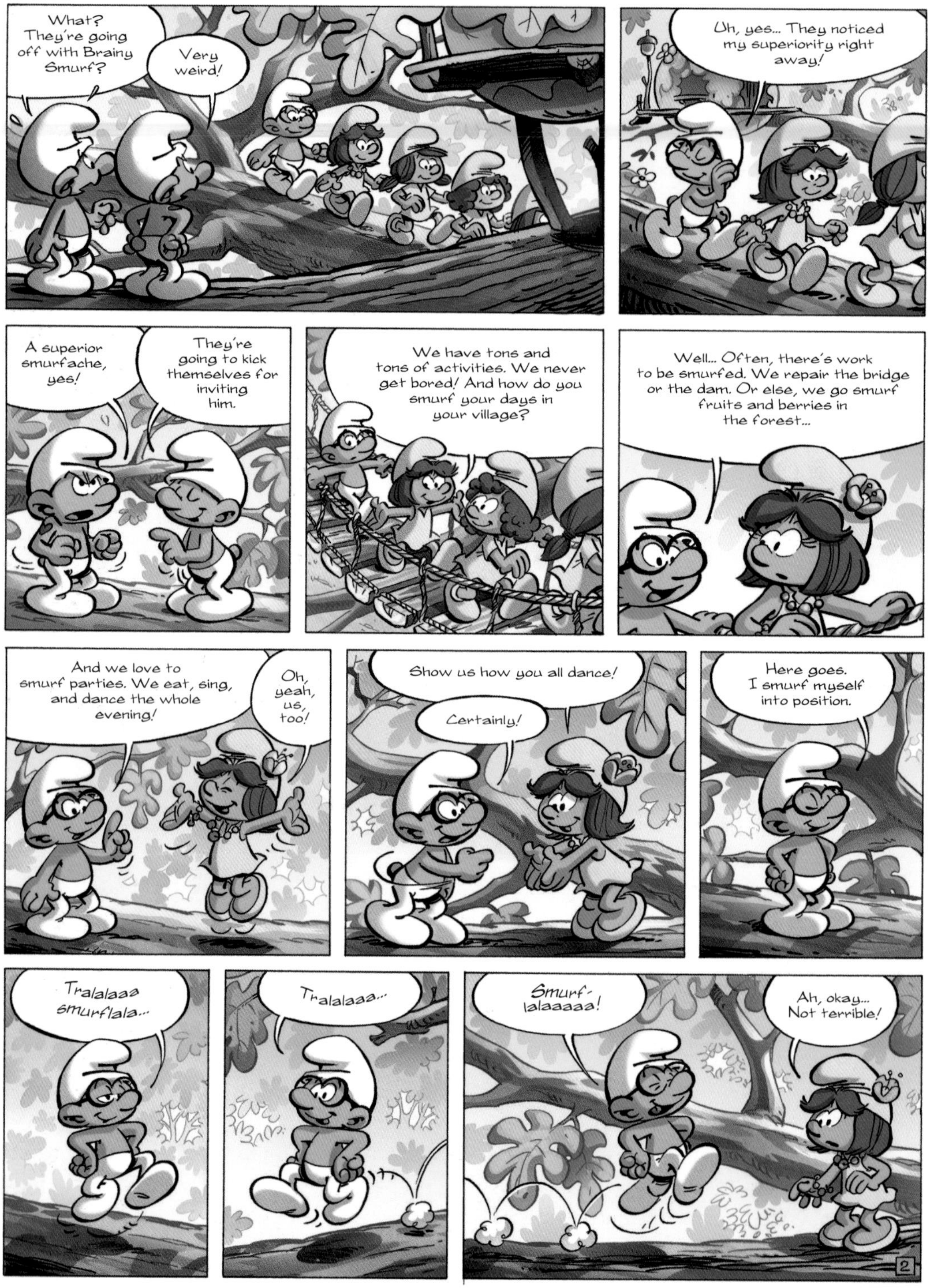

What? They're going off with Brainy Smurf?
Very weird!
Uh, yes... They noticed my superiority right away!
A superior smurfache, yes!
They're going to kick themselves for inviting him.
We have tons and tons of activities. We never get bored! And how do you smurf your days in your village?
Well... Often, there's work to be smurfed. We repair the bridge or the dam. Or else, we go smurf fruits and berries in the forest...
And we love to smurf parties. We eat, sing, and dance the whole evening!
Oh, yeah, us, too!
Show us how you all dance!
Certainly!
Here goes. I smurf myself into position.
Tralalaaa smurflala...
Tralalaaa...
Smurf-lalaaaaa!
Ah, okay... Not terrible!
2

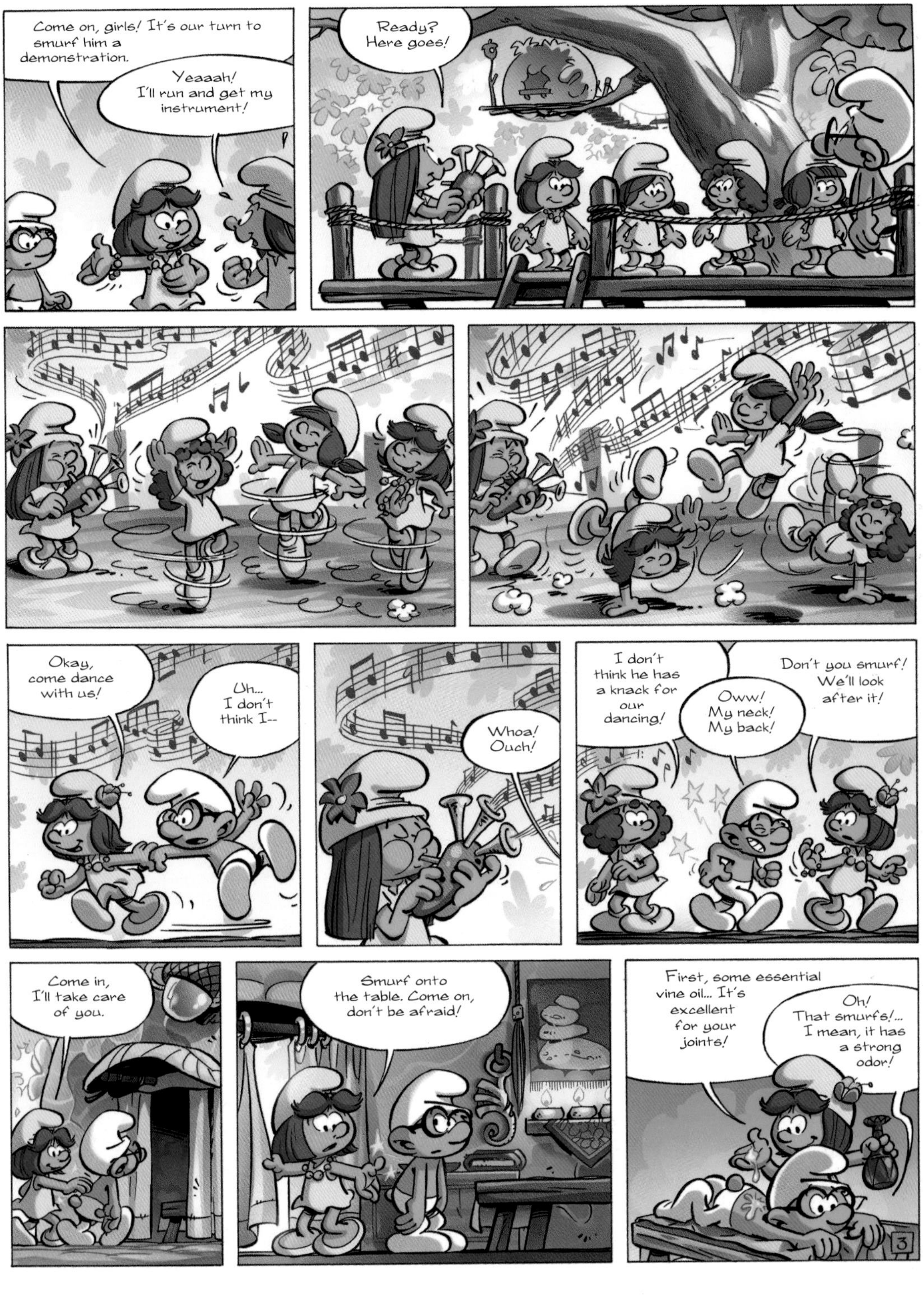

Come on, girls! It's our turn to smurf him a demonstration.
Yeaaah! I'll run and get my instrument!
Ready? Here goes!
Okay, come dance with us!
Uh... I don't think I--
Whoa! Ouch!
I don't think he has a knack for our dancing!
Oww! My neck! My back!
Don't you smurf! We'll look after it!
Come in, I'll take care of you.
Smurf onto the table. Come on, don't be afraid!
First, some essential vine oil... It's excellent for your joints!
Oh! That smurfs!... I mean, it has a strong odor!
3

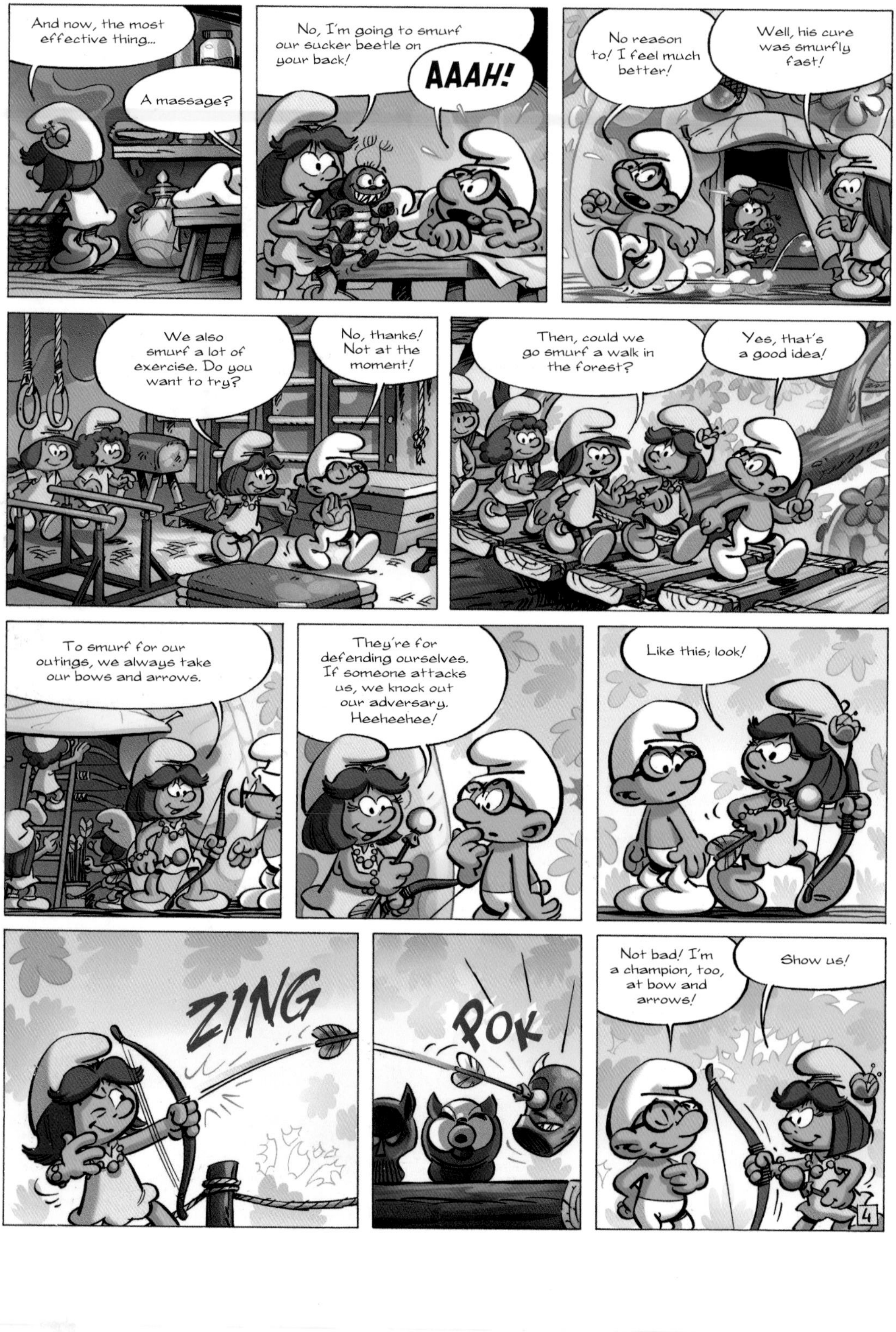
And now, the most effective thing...
A massage?
No, I'm going to smurf our sucker beetle on your back!
AAAH!
No reason to! I feel much better!
Well, his cure was smurfly fast!
We also smurf a lot of exercise. Do you want to try?
No, thanks! Not at the moment!
Then, could we go smurf a walk in the forest?
Yes, that's a good idea!
To smurf for our outings, we always take our bows and arrows.
They're for defending ourselves. If someone attacks us, we knock out our adversary. Heeheehee!
Like this; look!
ZING
POK
Not bad! I'm a champion, too, at bow and arrows!
Show us!
4